The Gingerbread Man

Retold by Mairi Mackinnon

Illustrated by
Elena Temporin

Reading Consultant: Alison Kelly
Roehampton University

This story is about

a little
old woman,

a little
old man,

a gingerbread man,

a horse, a cow,

a farmer,

some children   and a fox.

3

Once upon a time, a little old woman

and a little old man
lived on a farm.

5

Most of the time, they
were happy.

6

But one thing made
them sad.

They had no children.

So the little old woman decided to make a boy out of gingerbread.

She mixed the dough

and cut out a shape.

She gave him eyes

a mouth

and buttons

and put him in the oven
to bake.

11

Soon she could smell hot gingerbread.

She opened the oven
door and looked in.

And a gingerbread
man jumped out and
ran away.

"Stop!" shouted the
little old woman.
"Stop! Stop!" shouted
the little
old man.

But the gingerbread
man ran out of the
house, singing.

16

"Run, run, as fast as you can
You can't catch me
I'm the gingerbread man!"

The gingerbread man
ran past a horse and
a cow.

"Come here!"
said the cow.
"We want to eat you."

19

But the gingerbread
man ran on down the
road, singing.

"I have run away from
a little old woman and a
little old man, and I can run
away from you too!"

"Run, run, as fast as you can
You can't catch me
I'm the gingerbread man!"

The gingerbread
man ran past a farmer
in a field.

24

"Stop! Come here!" said the farmer. "I want to eat you."

But the gingerbread
man ran on down the
road, singing.

"I have run away from
a horse, a cow, a little old
woman and a little old man
and I can run away from
you too!"

"Run, run, as fast as you can
You can't catch me
I'm the gingerbread man!"

The gingerbread man
ran past a school full
of children.

"Come here!"
said the children.
"We want to eat you."

31

But the gingerbread
man ran on down the
road, singing.

"I have run away from a farmer, a horse, a cow, a little old woman and a little old man and I can run away from you too!"

"Run, run, as fast as you can
You can't catch me
I'm the gingerbread man!"

Then the gingerbread
man came to a river.

He wanted to cross it,
but he couldn't swim.

A fox saw him.

Mmm, you look good!

"I'll take you across," said the fox.

The gingerbread man
jumped on his tail.

The fox started
swimming but his tail
was in the water.

"I'm sorry," said the fox.
"My tail is getting wet."

The gingerbread man
climbed up the fox.

Water started creeping
up the fox's back.

"I'm sorry," said the fox.
"My back is getting wet."

Climb on to
my nose.

The gingerbread man
climbed up the fox.

S<small>N</small>A<small>P</small>! went the fox and
the gingerbread man was
a quarter gone.

SNAP! went the fox and
the gingerbread man
was half gone.

S_NA_P! went the fox and
the gingerbread man
was three quarters gone.

S_NA_P! GULP! And
that was the end of
the gingerbread man.

Series editor:
Lesley Sims

Designed by Louise Flutter
Cover design by Russell Punter

First published in 2006 by Usborne Publishing Ltd., Usborne House,
83-85 Saffron Hill, London EC1N 8RT, England. www.usborne.com
Copyright © 2006 Usborne Publishing Ltd.